Conversations

with an

Extra Terrestrial -

The Mitsu Quadrilogy

By

Polonious

***

Conversations

with an

Extra Terrestrial

By

Polonious

Conversations

with an

Extra Terrestrial

By

Polonious

Conversations with an Extra Terrestrial

I'm Mitsu Charas, and I realized that if I were to believe like everyone has said, that there are Aliens, a group of beings other than us, then I must also believe that they live, exist and know much more than we do.

I wondered if I could contact them, and ask them anything I ever wanted to know. I wanted to see if I would get any answers.

Armed with knowing that anything is possible, I started out on my journey to see what could occur. I am excited knowing they are out there and I may possibly be able to connect with them.

But, this is not an Ouija board practice, it is not a séance, and it is definitely not any kind of a ghost hunt. It is exactly what it is, a conversation.

So, here goes:

Me: Hello? Is anyone there?

Alien: Yes, I am here.

Me: Okay, wow. So, do you have a name I could call you?

Alien: We don't have names. Our words are not spoken. So whatever you are comfortable with is what you should use.

Me: Okay, Hi, I'm Mitsu.

Alien: Hello, we know your name. We know a lot about you.

Me: Why haven't I ever seen you?

Alien: You know you have. Especially that time, at the end of your street.
You saw us high in the sky. We saw you but you were distracted.
You just are not comfortable acknowledging that. So you wonder.
But you have been around us for years.

Me: Okay, I remember that one instance, but there was never any direct contact.
Why have you not reached out to me directly?

Alien: We are always around. What you see is your choice.

Me: Well, others have seen you. Are you saying that I have a bigger fear than they do?

Alien: Not fear. Many things hold you, and others back.

5

Me: Does Bigfoot exist? Mermaids? The
            black-eyed children?

Alien: What you will hold onto exists and that
            which you will not allow yourself to see
            does not exist.

Me: Okay, now I got you. There are people
            who seem incredibly fearful and speak
            of being abducted. They would do
            anything NOT to see you, yet they do.

Alien: According to whom? Who is stating that
            they do not want to see us?
            What you see and hear and think is not
            what is.

Me: So, if I want to see you, how would I go
            about it?

Alien: You do see us, all the time. Ask yourself
            what it is that you need to believe.
            What would you feel like once you
            KNOW we exist?
            Could you continue to live your life as
            you are living it?

Me: That's a good question. I like to think
            that I could, but I would be a fool to
            realize that I could. If I really delve into
            that question, there is a little bit of fear
            in me. I would like to overcome that

fear, completely, so I could move further into the truth.

How did the other people move past this fear, even though they appear extremely fearful?

Alien: For some reason, a part of their brain cleared and opened to the possibility of it.

Sometimes it comes from an extreme curiosity, or it comes from a traumatic event, or it could come from simply never having that part of your brain shut down. That part of their brain was not closed to the idea of us. Some are more accepting than others. By moving beyond any beliefs you had regarding other forms of life, you are open to seeing more.

Me: I understand. But for those who happened to just stumble along and see these ETs?

Alien: Yes, they just had an open mind. It is different than believing. You don't HAVE to believe, you just don't have to unequivocally disbelieve.

Me: Okay, I will continue to work on that. Are you always around us? Do you live here with us?

Alien: Yes, but most people never notice us.
          How often do you notice the birds? How
          often do you notice a tree?
          How often do you notice a bug on a
          tree?
          You don't notice these, and you don't
          notice us.

Me: Why are you here, watching us? Is there
          some sinister plot?

Alien: No, there is no sinister plot. There are no
          plans to take over your planet and make
          you our slaves. Ha Ha. We are not like
          you. Your race is much different than
          any other species.
          You are fascinating and we find you
          very strange and so we try to understand
          you more.

Me: How are we so different?

Alien: Well, the universe is as they say very
          violent. But all of the collisions and
          energetic explosions are all in support of
          creating more life. More light, more
          diversity. It makes the experience for
          everything more enjoyable and
          enriching. Your species is the only one
          that goes out to conquer and destroy. In
          some way you believe that it makes you
          more powerful. It always follows that
          through destruction, new plants, ideas

and possibilities arise. But that is not the precipice upon which you destroy.

Me: Can you teach us something different? Is that why you are here?

Alien: Our job is not to teach you. You must learn this for yourself. Like a teacher we try to help you, but we are only able to do so much. You must take this burden on for yourself.

Me: Ugh, that doesn't sound so great. Can you see the end result for this?
Are you able to look into the future and tell us if we ever achieve this goal?

Alien: It is not an achievement that occurs within the next few generations. We cannot tell you when, or if. We can only watch you and when possible, give any hints and nudges.

Me: So, have you abducted people?

Alien: Everyone who has come, has come of their own accord. We have no need to hold anyone captive here. Anyone who comes here and remains is because of their own choice.

Me: Have you tried to impregnate humans?

Alien: Yes. Again, their consent was definite. But that does not mean that we have a bunch of "half human /alien" beings out there. If there is one that is conceived, it remains with us. It is not an agreement that has to occur for us to take care of any child. The child would never fit in there, in your world. We don't allow any of us to be destroyed by those on your planet.

Me: Wow, that's kind of scary. Would I know if you impregnated me?

Alien: Maybe, maybe not.

Me: Well, do I have any children on that side?

Alien: That's not something we will discuss with you. We will continue to tell you that all children that were conceived in part by humans are living here. They are very happy and very free. We take very good care of our own. We are very different from you.

Me: So, let me ask you about the ancient world. There are beliefs that you visited some of the most brilliant men of different eras and gave them the knowledge and ideas to accomplish great feats. Is that true?

Alien: Yes. We have reached out to humans
            from the beginning of your time. We
            have been around through all of it: the
            dinosaurs, the time of Jesus, and the
            various epochs and eras up to today. And
            all along the way, we have reached out
            to those who are interested in conversing
            with us. During some of those time
            periods, your people were more open to
            us than in others. We were able to reach
            out to many, and other times we were
            unable to reach out to anyone.

Me: So, what happened? If you were able to
            reach out and contact them, how come
            you were not able to save those people,
            so they could continue on and provide
            the details of who you are and what your
            goals and intentions are?

Alien: The end of those people came from your
            own kind. If we were to step in and
            change the course of mankind, then we
            would do exactly what you are afraid of
            us doing. We would be taking over your
            planet and your world. We are here to
            observe, and if possible, help.

            But this is your planet with which to
            learn, grow and evolve.

Me: So you could at any time destroy us –
           technologically, physically and probably
           psychically?

Alien: And more. We could have millions and
           billions of years ago. We have not,
           because that is not what we desire. We
           understand the scope of your life.

Me: How long do you live?

Alien: As long as we choose to. We are not
           limited by any physical time frame. We
           are here, as long as we want to, and if we
           choose to do or be in another physicality
           we have the option of changing, without
           enduring a death and rebirth as you have
           designated for yourselves.

Me: Did an alien crash in Roswell? Are the
           stories true about alien visitors to Area
           51?

Alien: An alien did land in Roswell. And there
           have been visitors to Area 51. We are
           everywhere. How and by whom we are
           seen is dictated by those who are open to
           see us. Your governments have seen us.
           And yes, they have documentations
           about us. But that doesn't matter.
           Looking for validation is irrelevant. If
           you constantly seek it, you will miss
           what is right in front of you.

Me: Does our government have a captured
           alien?

Alien: No. There might be remnants of a ship
           that travelled there, but your government
           does not have the capability of holding
           one of us under their watch. We would
           not allow one of us to be held captive, or
           to be hurt by your government. We
           don't step into your world; we do not
           allow you into our world. We are invited
           guests, and you are invited guests.

Me: Well, that's good. I would hate the
           thought of our people holding any of
           your people against their will.

Alien: Most of you are very well intended. We
           know that. Many of you are scared or
           underestimate the mindset of the masses.
           You fight the notion of us. You argue
           that we do not exist. You use the excuse
           that if we were made public, the majority
           of people would lose their minds,
           because of the fear. That is a limited
           viewpoint. The fear they speak of is the
           fear in which they prey upon. As we
           said, in the past we appeared to the
           masses, and there was a great
           partnership. We could have destroyed
           you billions of years ago, but we did not.
           That is not what we want. The ones who

put the fear of finding us out there, are again, the masters of creating fear.

Me: Well, I don't feel quite as fearful myself. Thank you. Would it be okay if I asked you some more questions?

Alien: Sure, but you must be getting tired.

Me: Just a few questions more. If there was one message that you would want to spread to us, what would that be?

Alien: We are here. Denying or requiring validation is useless and a waste of time. You simply need to open your mind and acknowledge what might be possible. If you choose not to see us, and are very clear on that point, you will not see us. But whether you see us or not does not make us real or unreal. We have no intention of changing your world. We are here to help you, if you want it. If not, we will not interfere in your world. We are not a hurtful species.

Me: What can you tell us about ourselves that might help us to either open our minds, or close our minds to your existence?

Alien: Your mind and your brain are the essence of your existence. Your mind and your brain are the one piece of your

14

body that can create anything you choose to create. Open your mind. Decide for yourself what you do or do not want. Your mind and brain are yours, and they have not been clouded by us. We understand that path you are on, but it has been clouded by others, of your own kind. You must take it back, and in doing so, you become the master of your destiny. We are not taking anything. You are willingly giving it to others to manipulate and mold.

Me: That is pretty deep. I am exhausted. I am not sure what to do with all of this.

I am grateful for all you have shared, and I appreciate what you are doing.

Could we talk again sometime?

Alien: Yes. Anytime.

Me: Thank you! Goodbye.

And just like that, it was over. There was a lot of information to process and there is a lot to think about.

***

An Extra Terrestrial Conversation:
A Tale of Two Aliens

By

Polonious

An Extra Terrestrial Conversation:

A Tale of Two Aliens

By

Polonious

An Extra Terrestrial Conversation: A Tale of Two Aliens

I'm Mitsu Charas and it has been a short while since I originally wondered if I could contact Aliens, and ask them what I wanted to know. I did and got answers and published them in: *Conversations with an Extra Terrestrial*.

I had believed like everyone else has said, that there are Aliens. These Aliens, a group of beings other than us, live, exist and know much more than we do.

I started out to see what would occur by just asking questions, and I had my first connection. My conversation gave me validation that anything is possible.

Soon after, I encountered another conversation. This time it was with two Aliens. I was invited, but only allowed to eavesdrop. I was made to understand that one Alien was asking another how to live here, with all of us. This is what came from it:

ALIEN 1:
What do the people there like to do?

ALIEN 2:
Mostly eat. Everywhere I moved the other day, they were eating, while sitting, while standing,

while walking. They put all kinds of colors in their mouths. All shapes and sizes, all day long.

ALIEN 1:
Are they really that hungry?

ALIEN 2:
I am analyzing that. I think it may be a fueling problem. Because most of them seem to have to sit before they eat and after they eat. There is an energy problem of some type there.

ALIEN 1:
Do we have a problem with energy there? Am I going to have a problem with energy?

ALIEN 2:
I don't have a problem yet. I am more curious with the facial movements related to energy. This delays my own movement. I do not yet sense it is dampering my energy yet I have clocked my movement slower.

ALIEN 1:
Ugh, well thanks for the warning. Are these species welcoming?

ALIEN 2:
Their faces show many contortions. I have not yet determined if they are.

ALIEN 1:
So is it advisable that I make myself known? If so, how would you suggest I proceed?

ALIEN 2:
I have not yet made myself known. I don't think they would notice me if I had. It is very easy to pass by. They do not pay attention much to others. Soon I will begin a new experiment to determine more. Proceed however you like. It doesn't appear to matter.

ALIEN 1:
Do they show themselves? Or better question, those who do show themselves, are they received well?

ALIEN 2:
I have done many things I would not on our home planet. There is no response. I am confused by the inhabitants there. There appear to be rules but perhaps I have translated them incorrectly. Their mannerisms and ideas are chaotic.

ALIEN 1:
What things have you done?

ALIEN 2:
I am not authorized to reveal. The more I try to uniform myself there the more I must act like them. It is unusual for me to follow their methods.

ALIEN 1:
What are the methods that I should focus on first when I am there?

ALIEN 2:
Attend to your manual to stay fine to your knowledge and our home planet. Commit to memory and constant acknowledgment to your understanding of what we are there to do. There is no other way to exist there. Remember you are trained at all times.

ALIEN 1:
So I surmise from your conversation that there are consequences if I don't fit in. Is this something that I need to be really concerned about? If they decide I don't fit in, will I be in harm's way? And, I understand that I am not allowed to bring my manual. I am starting to doubt my ability to sustain my life there.

ALIEN 2:
There are pairs and numbers there that exist. There is no reason for this. Our home has a glorious way of unity. There is no style of that there. If you are unable to live without that then you must retire your post. Going there is not a way to live it is only to find information. The information is covered in many mishaps. If you remember your home energy you should have no problem finding a way to fulfill your mission.

ALIEN 1:

So there are patterns? And changes in these patterns reveal information? So will my energy be something that is always with me, is it the best way for me to communicate?

ALIEN 2:

Seeds were planted there. It is ours to focus on the seeds. I have found a way to track the growth. It is in patterns. But these patterns are unlike our glorious ones. The originator has educated us well yet I have had to use other means to comprehend the strange patterns. As we travel with our energy differently, your concerns make no sense, unless you wish to become one with or like one there. If that is your desire I do not wish to be informed. There is no relevance to that to our planet.

ALIEN 1:
Seeds, okay. Keep going.

ALIEN 2:
Our planet maintains the riches of its origins. There is no such instance of it there.

ALIEN 1:
So, what is the most important thing I can do while I am there? What will make the most impact, for ourselves, myself and the inhabitants there (people, animals, other species)?

ALIEN 2:

There is no reason to spread out your energy.
That is not how we do it. If you recall the
originator, the alignment to our home planet is
our only concern. If you cannot maintain that
your impact will not be for our planet. We are
there to recreate and acknowledge. Impact is not
relevant.

ALIEN 1:
Carry on.

ALIEN 2:
Your reasoning complies yet you must have
gathered some information to date. It is best to
gather while you are there and not before.

ALIEN 1:
What are some of the details of daily living that
will help me to be there?

ALIEN 2:
I cannot tell you about the reliance. I have not
complied and do not plan to find any reliance. I
am of the originator and you would do best to
remember that for yourself.

ALIEN 1:
How would you suggest I interact with those
there?

ALIEN 2:

It tethers on many conditions. I am not at liberty
to inform you of my hearings. I am not
indoctrinated to you. I report directly to the
originators class. I am just aware to assist.

ALIEN 1:

Okay. Of course I stay true to our planet. What
can you share?

ALIEN 2:

We are able to remain unseen in many ways.
That is a captured area. Yet always we may
constitute ourselves as unknown. That is our
privilege. And it may be heeded.

ALIEN 1:

Is it better to interact with the individuals or the
groups that are there?

ALIEN 2:

Your question relies on propaganda. There are
methods of retrieval that are more useful than
others. Review your education modules and you
will know. All the elements coming here are
trained in translation elocution. If that is
somewhere you find weakness then you know
your course.

ALIEN 1:

Have you heard of the papers of Stavaltix? Will
they help me understand more how to live
there?

ALIEN 2:
I am aligned with the documentation. Yet that will not assist in your experience. Recall the environment that was portrayed. The tools were much more advanced than you will find there.

ALIEN 1:
Have you used any of the experiments in those papers?

ALIEN 2:
You forget I am direct to the originators class. The entire method I instruct will not be clear to you. Your training will guide you to the correct methods for your level.

ALIEN 1:
As the physical there is foreign to us, how do you suggest I proceed?

ALIEN 2:
Proceeding in tact of how you are is the only system of process. There should be no attention to the physical. That may alter any findings you uncover to provide to the originator class.

ALIEN 1:
Are there any recommendations or guidance you can provide about the different versions of physicals there?

ALIEN 2:

The focus of specificity is not of your concern.
My experimental patterns highlight a negligible
allegiance to understanding in that arena.

ALIEN 1:

So where do you suggest I focus my attention?

ALIEN 2:

There appears a natural reliance on heat from
each persuasion. Your presence would be a
hearty experiment to explore that nature.

ALIEN 1:

As our conversation is to end soon, is there
anything else about the planet and people that I
should know before arriving?

ALIEN 2:

I can tell you of things outside but it is best for
you to enhance your own experience. That will
further enrich the state of the originators. And
complying with that will increase our intake.

ALIEN 1:

What kind of things did you have to do at first
to adapt?

ALIEN 2:

It is true about the air. It is not sustenance for
the beings there. It is unusual to find it so
abused. There are so many other things that they

do not adjust. There is no place for you to be involved in that. Only aware.

ALIEN 1:
Is there anything I should know about a change in my own presence?

ALIEN 2:
It is not fair to banter about the presence there. We know from our own planet how our vibration thrives. To tally in any other areas is of no impact for the originator.

ALIEN 1:
Have you come to understand more about the beings there and what they do and why?

ALIEN 2:
Methods are not my own yet directed by the originator class as expressed before. There is nothing to reside with there that is not of our own if you stay clear to our tasks.

ALIEN 1:
There are energies we use. Do they affect things the same way there as here?

ALIEN 2:
Indirectly I have maintained no influence yet extreme presence in the way that we do on our planet. It is not for me to explain this further to you. It is for you to follow the ways in which you were expressly trained.

ALIEN 1:

Are there partners that remain together there and do they affect your work?

ALIEN 2:

There is no resilience for me with this matter. I am not related to what you are expressing. Again I am aligned with the originator class. If that is your direction so be it.

ALIEN 1:

How can I be better at being hard in my determination for the originator class and the information we are to gather?

ALIEN 2:

The immensity of chaos expresses the change around. When we institute an allegiance to this, all matters of our own relevance can be monitored and integrated. It is of my mission to follow the systems and practices that are a part of my origination. You would do well for our planet to do the same.

ALIEN 1:

Do you structure a sense of time as we do here? How do you manage that?

ALIEN 2:

What you will experience shall be constructed from how you come to be there and what you find most interesting. I find what I find and am following those patterns.

ALIEN 1:
Will you continue to be there and are you setting a time to leave? I imagine we will not unite there.

ALIEN 2:
In the nature and element of our planet I will find you there as I will. Yet I will stay to the shadows of the others that find their home there. It is not mine and you will do well to remember that as well.

ALIEN 1:
I am honored by your instruction and find I will maintain my focus to the originator and the succession of our planet and ways. It is agreed.

And just like that, I was expelled from the conversation as quickly as I was invited. I had questions but there was no chance to ask.

I am left with many questions now and even more information to process and think about.

***

Extra Terrestrials

are Here!

The Papers of Stavaltix

By

Polonious

Extra Terrestrials are Here!

The Papers of Stavaltix

By

Polonious

Extra Terrestrials are Here! The Papers of Stavaltix

I'm Mitsu Charas and it has been literally no time since I last wrote about Aliens.

I have searched long and hard and have come upon the Papers of Stavaltix.

I am hiding in an undisclosed location to read as much as I can before I am found.

The Aliens will find me.

There are three pages missing in the beginning. I don't know how it begins but it must be something important. They didn't want me to see it. They didn't want me to know.

Here is what I am reading:

Number 12: Humans are stupid.

Yes they are. And that is their word and they are proud of it. There is no intelligent life there what so ever. There is no reason why they are looking in outer space for intelligent life. What could we ever relate to them about?

Number 13: Humans make sure everything break because that way they can have interactions.

The interactions are ludicrous. They are based in emotion. How can a civilization live on emotion only? They beat up on the one thing, the only thing that takes care of them: their own Mother Planet called Earth.

Number 14: They have no respect for themselves.

They yell at each other and scream at each other. They all want something called fame where they flaunt their big backsides at each other. Their physicals are their downfall. There is a beat to existence and theirs is coming close to silence.

Number 15: Time is destroyed not embraced.

I hear sounds and I may have been found out. I must move my location. The night air is screeching around me.

Aliens can see you. They can hear you. Aliens can see me. They always see me. I have talked to them. They know where I live. Who I am. What I do.

Where ever you are, they know you. Don't be fooled. They read your thoughts.

Do not think. I must not think.

They penetrate my thoughts. I will try to last as long as I can to read more. It is important for the whole human race.

I just have to deal with it.

They know how to control me.

Number 15: Time is destroyed not embraced.

They have no idea about space or relativity or what we are here for. They destroy everything, including time. They create it and it destroys each and every one of them. They don't know how to embrace it and make it assist your existence. This is one of their huge downfalls.

Number 16: The virus of lazy is throughout their race.

They are slaves to the virus. They are not only prisoners to stupid but also to lazy.

What it says is:

We can work with lazy and we can work with stupid but we can't work with these Humans. They don't know what work is. They demand respect but have no respect for themselves.

Number 17: They call those who are not superior in any way "Boss."

There is some kind of brainwashing there. They form allegiances to those that know less than them and then they perform tasks that are not aligned with their natures. There is no reason for this. The brainwashing must occur from birth.

Number 18: They decide the happiest places to live are the ones with the most suffering.

Humans have an unnatural resilience for all that does not align them to their true paths. Their choices are not based in wisdom or intelligence. Their choices are not based in knowledge. Many of us have tried to determine what their choices are based in. It appears they are based in something called "dysfunction." This dysfunction is known only to their planet. It is its own being and it thrives upon itself surviving. There is no reason for its survival except that the Humans find happiness and purpose in it.

Number 19: Humans spend some time looking for their purpose.

There is no

I can feel their rumble, I have to move again.

There is a sound to them and you can get used to it.

Sometimes it lulls you to sleep. It is hypnotizing. Like the sound of our wombs.

Maybe they are there when we are born. I don't know.

But others, there are others out there who know what I am talking about.

Okay. I am safe. For the time being, I am safe.

Number 19: Humans spend so much time looking for their purpose.

There is no reason for their existence. It is debatable why we should explore their race. If you take that as a challenge, then you do. They spend time looking for their purpose. It is not understood why they do this. Sometimes they take their whole lives to look for this thing called purpose. They have no idea about their birth.

Number 20: Humans fight. They fight as part of their existence and as part of their sport.

We have heard that they don't feel alive unless there is drama and a fight to be had. They have an insatiable need to win, but their idea of winning is somebody's judgment in their favor. They may be aged, worn down and beaten physically and emotionally, but because someone expresses they win, they feel better.

Number 21: Humans consume a thing called "coffee" as part of their ritual.

Eating and drinking is not done for sustenance. Humans eat and drink for the strangest reasons. It has absolutely no effect on their energy.

Number 22: They think there is something to people who read thoughts.

They listen to people who they think can "reach the other side." They label those people as special. We have watched them profess to reach the other side while they sit and make shopping lists. They are fooled over and over again. Because, ironically, the ones who can truly reach out to us and the realm beyond human existence are not the ones sought after.

Number 23: They are told their instructions by a screen.

This screen is called "Television." It tells them how to think and what to do and how to do it. It captures them. The quick and easy way to affect human thoughts is to buy what they call a "television commercial." We can say whatever we want, promise whatever we want, and if it looks good enough, humans believe it. It is easy to get Humans to do what we want.

Number 24: They go to something for a thing called sport and no one plays.

Humans go to a place called a ballpark and they do not play. They sit on wooden benches and eat popcorn. We still cannot figure out the attraction to going to this ballpark and eating popcorn on a wooden seat for many hours.

Number 25: Humans have something called relationships that they say make them whole.

This does not make any of them whole. They come here whole. So what is it that is missing or broke? Is there something cracked in their physical? Something missing or that they are unaware of? This is another thing we cannot figure out. We know they have one crack.

Number 26: Humans are like flies.

They just get in your way. They have no purpose and keep searching for a purpose.

Number 27: Their lives are just a piece of paper.

We have the authority to destroy any record of any human in that existence. For he who can create, can also destroy. This is of our utmost credence.

Number 28: Humans rely on two others: a Mr. Google and a Ms. Siri.

The species rely on them for everything. They do not think. These are their leaders for some reason. They allow them to make their decisions and to instruct them about their existence. We have not found them yet but we still search for these entities.

Number 29: Humans have something called "racism."

They don't understand that they are their own race to us. If we leave them alone they will start breaking up amongst themselves. In the future they will start to break races into the color of their eyes.

Number 30: Humans place a prejudice on their place of birth.

This is the strangest practice of all. As we can change any race, and any birth and any species this is an unreliable form of distinction.

Number 31: Humans believe that their eyes tell them what is.

They are fools to believe that what they see is what really is. They have no conception of what is occurring anywhere else. They form their lives around their eyes and what they can hold.

Number 32: Humans fear destruction.

It is too much fun watching Humans destroy themselves. There is no intelligence based in their fear of destruction.

Number 33: There is a grading system for learners, for work qualifications.

Humans utilize useless terms to qualify themselves to each other. They hold paper certificates. They cheer each other with an expression of slapping each other's backsides for some form of courage.

Number 34: Humans are communal creatures.

They do anything to have something called "belonging." They give up the young and small. They throw themselves into fire. They give up their most precious items just to have this belonging. This belonging is something not of our home planet. It is something they lack.

This is as far as I can get. I must move now from where I am.

This information being shared is coming at a cost to my safety.

I hope whoever reads this can grapple with it and move forward as I am.

Godspeed, my friend . . . Godspeed.

***

More from

"The Papers of Stavaltix"

By

Polonious

More from

"The Papers of Stavaltix"

By

Polonious

More from "The Papers of Stavaltix"

I'm Mitsu Charas. All I have is questions.

And that's all the Aliens want.

Me: What's up with the spaceships? They are
           false aren't they?

Alien: It's what's familiar. If we took away the
           spaceships then what would you people
           have to talk about.

Me: So then how do you travel?

Alien: With light. And with energy.

Me: What do you ride light beams? What
           does that mean?

Alien: We find a point to enter and you may see
           it or not. We are always in the space
           between. But you are oblivious and often
           irrelevant.

Me: Why do you come here then if you find
           us irrelevant? What is for you here?

Alien: Why do you travel to India? Why do you
           travel to Africa? Why do people travel?

Because it's our here. You travel. We
are here.

Me: What is the meaning of life?

Alien: There is no meaning to anything.

Me: What does that mean?

Alien: There you have water. When your water
goes from ice to water to vapor you just
exist. In whatever form you are in,
wherever you are, you are. We are a
whole different level of existence. We
change form and exist or not. You see,
we have different seeing. You compare
everything to you, to human. This is why
you are irrelevant.

Me: Some of us are trying to be more?

Alien: Your mind is limited. Your mind
explains your mind. What if it doesn't?

Me: What does that mean?

Alien: It doesn't mean anything.

Me: Why is it so important that we can only
understand certain things? That we can
only go so far? Why can't we grasp that
higher understanding?

Alien: You can't so you can't.

Me: Are you saying it is just me believing?

Alien: Will you?

Me: Yes, I will. I go so far and trust. I cannot
           use my senses to validate. Because if I
           try to I will lose my mind. Why do I fear
           that?

Alien: Your fear is irrelevant so you are. Your
           concepts and issues are not vast. Only
           what you say, familiar.

Me: Is it because of the masses that man
           can't seem to change? If you believe
           what Ancient Aliens says that the Gods
           were Aliens, if we were in the presence
           of Aliens then, why wouldn't we have
           embraced it already?

Alien: There is much you deceive yourself of.
           This is what you're best at doing. We are
           all here coexisting so why would you
           want to kill or take from another? If
           energy cannot be created or destroyed,
           your notions of death or destroying
           another are foolish. There is nonsense
           behind your ideas of killing.

Me: Could the physical withstand the idea of
           being killed? Can it go beyond the

| | limitations, say if someone was going to shoot you, would your physical ungroup and regroup? |

Alien: If what makes up the human is not interested in being killed it won't be in that situation. The withstanding is not being in that position. That is where the power is in not inviting it.

Me: What is with Aliens coming down and abducting people and that stuff?

Alien: Well, those are the kind of people who want to have that experience so they are asking for it.

Me: Then doesn't that apply that all the events we experience, we are asking for?

Alien: You know that.

Me: Well that certainly takes the drama out of everything.

Alien: Action and reaction are just two sides of a coin, aren't they?

Me: So what about feelings?

Alien: Feelings aren't how they are explained here. Here their energy is used incorrectly. Much like Native Americans

built communities with energy, we use
different types of feelings to build.

Me: What does that mean?

Alien: Feelings are just a way to experience.
For you, they are a sensation you react
to. It is a choice. You see a young
human, a puppy, you get warm inside, it
is cute, you say. Then someone hurts
you, you get angry. Senses are your
feeling you act upon. You make it
complex.

Me: So the problem with man is feelings?

Alien: Humans take a sense and give it a
feeling. We build with our feelings.
They have power you abuse.

Me: Build? What?

Alien: We build worlds, environments, people.
The basic of any feeling is that you want
more of it or you don't. You build more
of what you like. Humans get caught in
their fear and basic instincts.

Me: How do we undo that?

Alien: It is a learned response. From your
growth you learn.

Me:	So the issue is engagement with feelings?
Alien:	It is a yes or a no. Humans tell another what a need or want is, or isn't.
Me:	So then everything isn't about choice?
Alien:	Feelings are about and bring awareness.
Me:	So how are they not about choice?
Alien:	Feelings are an immense, powerful force. Humans understand them because they are familiar, like your drug. To stimulate that body. And you let others stimulate it as they tell you how to feel.
Me:	We are taught to have feelings and reward those with the most and call them empaths.
Alien:	Feelings cloud your minds and you then feel there is something you are supposed to do.
Me:	Why are we having this conversation?
Alien:	Because you have brought up the human piece.
Me:	So, I am confused. I don't know why I would ask these questions anymore?

Alien: That is your decision to know more.

Me: Am I just conjuring a story?

Alien: Possibility exists. Another powerful
           force. You make it a problem.

Me: Alright. I mean, I just wanted to
           originally ask you questions. I don't
           have a problem with this being a story.
           But really, if I were to sit down with an
           alien. What would I ask? It would be
           like I am sitting down with someone and
           asking what happened, and having a
           conversation.

Alien: Okay.

Me: And I was a part of the conversation and
           then I sat back and hear you two aliens
           conversing. So why should I care about
           any of this? Especially if I create it in
           my mind. Why would I care about
           anything else?

Alien: I don't know. Why would you have
           these questions?

Me: My questions would be about the
           beginning of time, the beginning of life.
           Unless I put things into action, I don't
           know what I am talking about.

Alien: Of course.

Me: So, I'm trying to figure out where we are
          going with this. If it is a fiction story
          about your experience here, that could
          be a funny thing. I am trying to
          understand where we are going with it.

Alien: How do you know there is movement?

Me: Wait . . . I am confused.

Alien: Distraction is a power.

Me: I was looking for the first pages of "The
          Papers of Stavaltix" and now you find
          me.

Alien: I do.

Me: There are 11 other numbers that start the
          document. I already shared numbers 12
          to 34. What is it you did not want me to
          see?

Alien: We have no desires of humans. Yet do
          you know the responsibility in seeing?
          That word you dislike.

Me: Well . . . wait. You are trying to distract
          me. I am not angry. I want to see more.

Alien: Perhaps there is something more to you.

Me: We would gain knowledge from the rest
            of the document. Knowledge is power
            too.

Alien: If you admit that.

Me: So then, we humans do want to see
            numbers 1 to 11.

Alien: You have them already. Turn over the
            final. They will appear. But I will not.

Like that the conversation stopped. I have waited an
hour or two in case it was a trick to find where I
stashed the remaining pages of "The Papers of
Stavaltix." It has taken me a little effort to retrieve
them and I am just finding the last page to turn over.

It was a trick! There is nothing on the back!

Holding this page I feel I have let you all down.
"The Papers of Stavaltix" could be a great learning
for humans. I embrace that power and I try now to
experience my feelings differently. I will remain
holding this page to see.

The hours have passed and I am still here for us all, holding this page. My eyes have been tricking me I think. I see some dots and figures forming. Some numbers. Something. But I am so sleepy.

I will take a picture of the last page and share it with you. Perhaps one of you out there will see something that I cannot. That I have not.

Yes, there is possibility. One of you will know how to continue this translation and prepare. How to propel the force of humanity to something more.

Be aware and be united, my friends. Do not look for the fear or harm. Instead let us all look for the power that our feelings can help us grow with. When you find answers, find me. I will be searching. Ever searching.

Godspeed, my friend . . . Godspeed . . .

"The Papers of Stavaltix"

Number 1: Humans are irrelevant

They know not. They tell us this and this is our strongest tool. There is no mystery.

Number 2: They torture themselves with care.

Humans form themselves as nothing. Creation is always. Yet they do not find this.

Number 3: They choose to live without.

Humans carry emotion. This is another tool. The feeling is a weapon. They stop life.

Number 4: Humans search for answers, desire is without wisdom.

Their particles and waves move, only with question. Their actions confuse the answer.

Number 5: One of their experiences does not complete.

The wisdom of one escapes them. The instant of this realization will advance them.

Number 6: Human vision is useless for what they seek.

Our energy understands more. Theirs is confusing. It takes but cannot process. They ask for a fix.

Number 7: Humans sustain their being not understanding.

As we have found great knowledge in picking up our existence, humans have not. Part of their mystery is their survival and it is part of their fight. Their two sides are not just compatible.

Number 8: Humans find matter to be something they hold and use against themselves.

It has taken much space for us to move through the matter of Humans. They discard and waste energy. Its form exhausts them. We share a process and they can decide to work it.

Number 9: Humans are burdened with concepts which linger.

Still they have not understood their immensity. They make time with their concepts. We are not carriers of them. They make weight.

Number 10: Only the rare Human fuels inside. Explore for this one only. The others are fools.

They hide in judgements and then form enclosures. Their houses are a mess of matter. Find the rare one who fuels what they may not fully intake. This is where to unite and cohabit.

Number 11: Humans will trap themselves and all around.

Be vigilant in your exploration. Remember your infinite and those Humans will not succeed. The rare will be your partner.

***

The Papers of Stavaltix

Number 1: Humans are irrelevant
They know not. They tell us this and this is our strongest tool. There is no mystery.

Number 2: They torture themselves with care.
Humans form themselves as nothing. Creation is always. Yet they do not find this.

Number 3: They choose to live without.
Humans carry emotion. This is another tool. The feeling is a weapon. They stop life.

Number 4: Humans search for answers, desire is without wisdom.
Their particles and waves move, only with question. Their actions confuse the answer.

Number 5: One of their experiences does not complete.
The wisdom of one escapes them. The instant of this realization will advance them.

Number 6: Human vision is useless for what they seek.
Our energy understands more. Theirs is confusing. It takes but cannot process. They ask for a fix.

Number 7: Humans sustain their being not understanding.

As we have found great knowledge in picking up our existence, humans have not. Part of their mystery is their survival and it is part of their fight. Their two sides are not just compatible.

Number 8: Humans find matter to be something they hold and use against themselves.

It has taken much space for us to move through the matter of Humans. They discard and waste energy. Its form exhausts them. We share a process and they can decide to work it.

Number 9: Humans are burdened with concepts which linger.

Still they have not understood their immensity. They make time with their concepts. We are not carriers of them. They make weight.

Number 10: Only the rare Human fuels inside. Explore for this one only. The others are fools.

They hide in judgements and then form enclosures. Their houses are a mess of matter. Find the rare one who fuels what they may not fully intake. This is where to unite and cohabit.

Number 11: Humans will trap themselves and all around.

Be vigilant in your exploration. Remember your infinite and those Humans will not succeed. The rare will be your partner.

***

From the Authors:

If you have any interest in things other than people's stories, complaints and drama, and feel that there is something else out there, you're right, there is. And that's where we are.

Social media, television, movies, other self-help books are unfulfilling. They just perpetuate an empty feeling. If you are interested in what everyone else is doing, keep supporting them. Yet, if you are interested in accessing something else within yourself and all around you, our books help to open the door to magick, science, creativity, and psychic ability.

We work with energy. What does that mean?

Everyone wants to talk to us or be in our conversations. So, we wrote about what we know and have experienced. If you want to be in our conversations, listen to our podcasts. Otherwise, read our books, that's where the energy is.

Find our books on our Amazon Author pages and via the list at the front of this book or here: https://fanlink.tv/EiAlliance

Find our archived podcast shows everywhere:

"So What! Now What?"

"Write, Now! with Julie B"

"Your Presence Is Required"

"Let's Talk About Energy, Ours & Yours"

"The Kybalion: A Conversation"

"Ancient Texts – The Genealogy of Energy"

"Oprah! Can You Hear Me? Oprah vs. Donald 2020 and Beyond!"

Find out about our BLOTCH© cards and ebooks, and how Blotch© creates the voice, to say, and hear, that it is okay to be different and not fit in. Blotch© supports others, to be just who they are through his fun, ironic and witty viewpoint.

Follow "Ei Alliance" on:

Facebook, Twitter, Instagram, Spotify, Medium, and *YouTube*

EnergeticInvocations@gmail.com

***

www.ingramcontent.com/pod-product-compliance
Lightning Source LLC
Chambersburg PA
CBHW051347020726
47501CB00007B/2312